DOVER · THRIFT · EDITIONS

Tartuffe

MOLIÈRE

DOVER PUBLICATIONS, INC.
Mineola, New York

DOVER THRIFT EDITIONS

GENERAL EDITOR: PAUL NEGRI
EDITOR OF THIS VOLUME: JOHN BERSETH

Bibliographical Note

This Dover edition, first published in 2000, contains the unabridged text of *Tartuffe*, based on the 18th-century translation from the French by H. Baker and J. Miller. A new Note has been added.

Library of Congress Cataloging-in-Publication Data

Molière, 1622–1673.
    [Tartuffe. English]
    Tartuffe / Molière.
       p. cm. — (Dover thrift editions)
    ISBN 0-486-41117-6 (pbk.)
     I. Title. II. Series.
PQ1842 .A42 2000
842'.4—dc21

99-044074

Manufactured in the United States of America
Dover Publications, Inc., 31 East 2nd Street, Mineola, N.Y. 11501

Note

"MOLIÈRE" was the pseudonym of the French actor-manager and dramatist Jean Baptiste Poquelin (1622–1673). Born in Paris and educated at the Jesuit College de Clermont, Molière abandoned his studies and the prospect of a court appointment to form the company of the Illustre Theatre in 1643. The troupe was not a great success during its two years in the capital—a time when Molière was imprisoned for nonpayment of debts—and began touring the French provinces in 1645. During the next dozen or so years Molière developed his theatrical skills to a high degree. His by-now polished company returned to Paris in 1658, under the patronage of Philippe, duc d'Orleans (the brother of King Louis XIV), and performed regularly before enthusiastic audiences. After a series of successful runs at the Petit-Bourbon, the company moved to the Palais-Royal in 1661. The company became the Troupe du roi in 1665.

Le Tartuffe ou l'imposteur was first performed at Versailles for the king in 1664. This three-act version was then performed only sporadically over the next three years, because of objections to its content by religious critics. In fact, no play of Molière's got him into such trouble with those in power. He persisted, however, and presented an expurgated version of *Tartuffe* at the Palais-Royal in 1667. The play in its final form, the one we know today, was first performed in 1669. In this production Molière played Orgon and his wife, Armande Bejart, played Elmire. In the original French the play, like most of Molière's work, was written in verse. The translation chosen for this edition, by W. Baker and J. Miller, does not keep to the rhyming or even the versification, but renders the French into poetic English prose that is faithful to the spirit and beauty of the playwright's original work.

Contents

Dramatis Personnae

MADAME PERNELLE — *Orgon's mother*
ORGON — *Elmire's husband*
ELMIRE — *Orgon's wife*
DAMIS — *Orgon's son*
MARIANE — *Orgon's daughter*
VALÈRE — *Mariane's suitor*
CLÉANTE — *Orgon's brother-in-law*
TARTUFFE — *bogus holy man*
DORINE — *waiting-maid to Mariane*
M. LOYAL — *a bailiff*
A POLICE OFFICER
FLIPOTE — *Madame Pernelle's maid*

The scene is in Paris, in Orgon's house

Act I.

Scene I.

MADAME PERNELLE, ELMIRE, MARIANE,
DAMIS, CLÉANTE, DORINE, FLIPOTE.

MME. PERNELLE.   Come Flipote, let's be gone, that I may get rid of them.

ELMIRE.   You walk so fast that one has much ado to follow you.

MME. PERNELLE.   Stay, daughter, stay; come no farther; this is all needless ceremony.

ELMIRE.   We only acquit ourselves of our duty to you; but pray, mother, what makes you in such haste to leave us?

MME. PERNELLE.   Because I can't endure to see such management, and nobody takes any care to please me. I leave your house, I tell you, very ill edified; my instructions are all contradicted. You show no respect for anything amongst you, every one talks aloud there, and the house is a perfect Dover Court.

DORINE.   If—

MME. PERNELLE.   You are, sweetheart, a noisy and impertinent Abigail, and mighty free of your advice on all occasions.

DAMIS.   But—

MME. PERNELLE.   In short, you are a fool, child; 'tis I tell you so, who am your grandmother; and I have told my son your father, a hundred times, that you would become a perfect rake and would be nothing but a plague to him.

MARIANE.   I fancy—

MME. PERNELLE.   Good-lack, sister of his, you act the prude, and look as if butter would not melt in your mouth; but still waters, they say, are always deepest, and under your sly airs you carry on a trade I don't at all approve of.

ELMIRE.   But mother—

1

MME. PERNELLE. By your leave, daughter, your conduct is absolutely wrong in everything; you ought to set them a good example, and their late mother managed 'em much better. You are a sorry economist, and what I can't endure, dress like any princess. She who desires only to please her husband, daughter, needs not so much finery.

CLÉANTE. But madame, after all—

MME. PERNELLE. As for you, sir, her brother, I esteem you very much, I love and respect you; but yet, were I in my son's her husband's place, I should earnestly entreat you not to come within our doors. You are always laying down rules of life that good people should never follow. I talk a little freely to you, but 'tis my humour; I never chew upon what I have at heart.

DAMIS. Your Monsieur Tartuffe is a blessed soul, no doubt—

MME. PERNELLE. He's a good man, and should be listened to; I can't bear, with patience, to hear him cavilled at by such a fool as you.

DAMIS. What! shall I suffer a censorious bigot to usurp an absolute authority in the family? And shall not we take the least diversion, if this precious spark thinks not fit to allow of it?

DORINE. If one were to hearken to him, and give in to his maxims, we could do nothing but what would be made a crime of; for the critical zealot controls everything.

MME. PERNELLE. And whatever he controls is well controlled. He would fain show you the way to Heaven; and my son ought to make you all love him.

DAMIS. No, look you, madame, neither father nor anything else can oblige me to have any regard for him. I should belie my heart to tell you otherwise. To me his actions are perfectly odious; and I foresee that, one time or other, matters will come to extremity between that wretch and me.

DORINE. 'Tis downright scandalous to see an upstart take on him at that rate here. A vagabond that had not a pair of shoes to his feet when he came hither, and all the clothes on his back would not fetch sixpence, that he should so far forget himself as to contradict everything and to play the master.

MME. PERNELLE. Mercy on me! Matters would go much better, were everything managed by his pious directions.

DORINE. He passes for a saint in your imagination; but, believe me, all he does is nothing but hypocrisy.

MME. PERNELLE. What a tongue!

DORINE. I would not trust him without good security, any more than I would his man Laurence.

MME. PERNELLE. What the servant may be at bottom, I can't tell; but I'll answer for the master that he is a good man; you wish him ill, and reject him, only because he tells you the naked truth. 'Tis sin that his heart can't brook, and the interest of Heaven is his only motive.

DORINE.   Ay; but why, for some time past, can't he endure that anybody should come near us? How can a civil visit offend Heaven, so much that we must have a din about it, enough to stun one? Among friends, shall I give you my opinion of the matter? [*Pointing to* ELMIRE] I take him, in troth, to be jealous of my lady.

MME. PERNELLE.   Hold your peace, and consider what you say. He is not the only person who condemns these visits. The bustle that attends the people you keep company with, these coaches continually planted at the gate, and the noisy company of such a parcel of footmen disturb the whole neighbourhood. I am willing to believe there's no harm done; but then it gives people occasion to talk, and that is not well.

CLÉANTE.   Alas, madame, will you hinder people from prating? It would be a very hard thing in life, if for any foolish stories that might be raised about people, they should be forced to renounce their best friends; and suppose we should resolve to do so, do you think it would keep all the world from talking? There's no guarding against calumny. Let us therefore not mind silly tittle-tattle, and let's endeavour to live innocently ourselves, and leave the gossiping part of mankind to say what they please.

DORINE.   May not neighbour Daphne and her little spouse be the persons who speak ill of us? People whose own conduct is the most ridiculous are always readiest to detract from that of others. They never fail readily to catch at the slightest appearance of an affair, to set the news about with joy, and to give things the very turn they would have them take. By colouring other people's actions like their own, they think to justify their conduct to the world, and fondly hope, by way of some resemblance, to give their own intrigues the air of innocence or to shift part of the blame elsewhere, which they find falls too hard upon themselves.

MME. PERNELLE.   All these arguments are nothing to the purpose. Orante is known to lead an exemplary life, her care is all for Heaven; and I have heard say that she has but an indifferent opinion of the company that frequents your house.

DORINE.   An admirable pattern indeed! She's a mighty good lady, and lives strictly, 'tis true, but 'tis age that has brought this ardent zeal upon her; and we know that she's a prude in her own defence. As long as 'twas in her power to make conquests, she did not balk any of her advantages; but when she found the lustre of her eyes abate, she would needs renounce the world that was on the point of leaving her; and under the specious mask of great prudence, conceals the decay of her worn-out charms. That is the antiquated coquettes' last shift. It is hard upon them to see themselves deserted by all their gallants. Thus forsaken, their gloomy disquiet can find no relief but in prudery; and then the severity of these good ladies censures all and forgives none. They cry out aloud upon every one's way of living, not out of a principle of charity, but envy, as not being able to suffer that another should taste those pleasures which people on the decline have no relish for.

MME. PERNELLE. [*To* ELMIRE] These are the idle stories that are told to please you, daughter. There's no getting in a word at your house, for madame here engrosses all the talk to herself. But I shall also be heard in my turn. I tell you my son never acted a wiser part than when he took this devout man into his family; that Heaven in time of need sent him hither to reclaim your wandering minds; that 'tis your main interest to hearken to his counsels, and that he reproves nothing that is not blameable. These visits, balls, and assemblies are all the inventions of the wicked spirit; there's not one word of godliness to be heard at any of them, but idle stuff, nonsense, and tales of a tub, and the neighbours often come in for a share; there's nobody they'll stop at to vilify. In short, the heads of reasonable people are turned by the confusion of such meetings. A thousand different fancies are started about less than nothing; and as a good doctor said the other day very well, 'Tis a perfect Tower of Babel, for every one here babbles out of all measure. Now to give you an account of where all this comes in. . . . [*Pointing to* CLÉANTE] What! is that spark giggling already? Go look for your fool to make a jest of, and unless—[*To* ELMIRE] Good-bye t'ye, daughter, I shall say no more. Depend on it, I have not half the esteem for your house I had, and it shall be very fine weather when I set my foot in your doors again. [*Giving* FLIPOTE *a box on the ear*] Come, you, you're dreaming and gaping at the crows; i'fakins! I'll warm your ears for you. Let's march, trollop, let's march.

Scene II.

CLÉANTE, DORINE.

CLÉANTE. I won't go, for fear she should fall foul on me again. That this good old lady—

DORINE. 'Tis pity, truly, she does not hear you call her so; she'd give you to understand how she liked you, and that she was not old enough to be called so yet.

CLÉANTE. What a heat has she been in with us about nothing! And how fond does she seem of her Tartuffe!

DORINE. Oh! truly, all this is nothing compared to the infatuation of her son, and were you to see him you'd say he was much worse. His behaviour in our public troubles had procured him the character of a man of sense, and of bravery for his prince; but he's grown quite besotted since he became fond of Tartuffe. He calls him brother, and loves him in his heart a hundred times better than either mother, son, daughter, or wife. He's the only confidant of all his secrets, and the wise director of all his actions; he caresses, he embraces him, and I think one could not have more affection for a mistress. He will have him seated at the upper end of the table, and is delighted to see him gobble as much as half a dozen. He must be helped to all the tit-bits, and whenever he but belches, he bids G—d bless him. In short, he dotes upon him, he's his all, his hero; he admires all he does, quotes him on all occasions, looks on every trifling action of his as a wonder, and every word an oracle. At the same time the fellow, knowing his blind side and willing to make the most on't, has a hundred tricks to impose upon his judgment and get his money from him in the way of bigotry. He now pretends truly to take the whole family to task; even the awkward fool his foot-boy takes upon him to lecture us with his fanatic face, and to demolish our patches, paint, and ribbons. The rascal, the other day, tore us a fine handkerchief that lay in the *Pilgrim's Progress*, and cried that it was a horrid profanation to mix hellish ornaments with sanctified things.

Scene III.

ELMIRE, MARIANE, DAMIS, CLÉANTE, DORINE.

ELMIRE.   [*To* CLÉANTE] You are very happy in not having come to the harangue she gave us at the gate. But I saw my husband, and as he did not see me, I'll go up to wait his coming.

CLÉANTE.   I'll wait for him here by way of a little amusement, only bid him good-morrow.

DAMIS.   Hint something to him about my sister's wedding; I suspect that Tartuffe's against it, and that he puts my father upon these tedious evasions; you are not ignorant how nearly I am concerned in it. If my friend Valère and my sister are sincerely fond of one another, his sister, you know, is no less dear to me, and if it must—

DORINE.   Here he is.

Scene IV.

ORGON, CLÉANTE, DORINE.

ORGON.   Hah! brother, good-morrow.

CLÉANTE.   I was just going, and am glad to see you come back. The country at present is not very pleasant.

ORGON.   Dorine. [*To* CLÉANTE] Brother, pray stay; you'll give me leave just to inquire the news of the family; I can't be easy else. [*To* DORINE] Have matters gone well the two days I have been away? What has happened here? How do they all do?

DORINE.   My lady the day before yesterday had a fever all day, and was sadly out of order with a strange headache.

ORGON.   And Tartuffe?

DORINE.   Tartuffe? Extremely well, fat, fair, and fresh-coloured.

ORGON.   Poor man!

DORINE.   At night she had no stomach, and could not touch a bit of supper, the pain in her head continued so violent.

ORGON.   And Tartuffe?

DORINE.   He supped by himself before her, and very heartily ate a brace of partridge, and half a leg of mutton hashed.

ORGON.   Poor man!

DORINE.   She never closed her eyes, but burnt so that she could not get a wink of sleep; and we were forced to sit up with her all night.

ORGON.   And Tartuffe?

DORINE.   Being agreeably sleepy, he went from table to his chamber, and so into a warm bed, and slept comfortably till next morning.

ORGON.   The poor man!

DORINE.   At length my lady, prevailed upon by our persuasions, resolved to be let blood; then she soon grew easier.

ORGON.   And Tartuffe?

DORINE.   He plucked up his spirit, as he should; and fortifying his mind against all evils, to make amends for the blood my lady lost, drank at breakfast four swingeing draughts of wine.

ORGON.   The poor man!

DORINE.   At present they both are pretty well, and I shall go before and let my lady know how glad you are of her recovery.

Scene V.

ORGON, CLÉANTE.

CLÉANTE.   She jokes upon you, brother, to your face; and without any design of making you angry, I must tell you freely that 'tis not without reason. Was ever such a whim heard of? Is it possible that a man can be so bewitching at this time of day as to make you forget everything for him? That after having, in your own house, relieved his indigence, you should be ready to—

ORGON. Hold there, brother, you don't know the man you speak of.

CLÉANTE. Well, I don't know him, since you will have it so. But then, in order to know what a man he is,—

ORGON. Brother, you would be charmed did you know him, and there would be no end of your raptures. He's a man—that—ah—a man—a man, in short, a man. Who always practises as he directs, enjoys a profound peace, and regards the whole world no more than so much dung. Ay, I am quite another man by his conversation. He teaches me to set my heart upon nothing; he disengages my mind from friendships or relations; and I could see my brother, children, mother, wife, all expire, and not regard it more than this.

CLÉANTE. Humane sentiments, brother, I must confess!

ORGON. Ah! had you but seen him as I first met with him, you would have loved him as well as I do. He came every day to church with a composed mien, and kneeled down just against me. He attracted the eyes of the whole congregation by the fervency with which he sent up his prayers to Heaven. He sighed and groaned very heavily, and every moment humbly kissed the earth. And when I was going out, he would advance before and offer me holy water at the door. Understanding by his boy (who copied him in everything) his low condition and who he was, I made him presents; but he always modestly would offer to return me part. 'Tis too much, he'd say, too much by half. I am not worth your pity. And when I refused to take it again, he would go and give it among the poor before my face. At length Heaven moved me to take him home, since which everything here seems to prosper. I see he reproves without distinction; and that even with regard to my wife, he is extremely cautious of my honour. He acquaints me who ogles her, and is six times more jealous of her than I am. But you can hardly imagine how very good he is. He calls every trifle in himself a sin; he's scandalised at the smallest thing imaginable, so far that the other day he told me he had caught a flea as he was at his devotions, and had killed it, he doubted, in rather too much anger.

CLÉANTE. 'Sdeath! you must be mad, brother, I fancy; or do you intend to banter me by such stuff? What is it you mean? All this fooling—

ORGON. Brother, what you say savours of libertinism. You are a little tainted with it; and, as I have told you more than once, you'll draw down some heavy judgment on your head one day or other.

CLÉANTE. This is the usual strain of such as you. They would have everybody as blind as themselves. To be clear-sighted is libertinism, and such as don't dote upon empty grimaces have neither faith nor respect to sacred things. Come, come, all this discourse of yours frights not me; I know what I say, and Heaven sees my heart. We are not to be slaves to your men of form. There are pretenders to devotion as well as to courage. And as we never find the truly brave to be such as make much noise wheresoever they are led by honour, so the good and truly pious, who are worthy of our imitation, are never those that deal much in grimace. Pray, would you make no distinction between hypocrisy and true devotion? Would you term them both alike, and pay the same regard to the mask as you do to the face? Would you put artifice on the level with sincerity, and confound appearance with reality? Is the phantom of the same esteem with you as the figure? and is bad money of the same value as good? Men generally are odd creatures. They never keep up to true nature. The bounds of reason are too narrow for them. In every character they overact their parts, and the noblest designs very often suffer in their hands because they will be running things into extremes and always carry things too far. This, brother, by the by.

ORGON.   Yes, yes, you are without doubt a very reverend doctor; all the knowledge in the world lies under your cap. You are the only wise and discerning man, the oracle, the Cato of the present age; all men, compared to you, are downright fools.

CLÉANTE.   No, brother, I am none of your reverend sages, nor is the whole learning of the universe vested in me; but I must tell you I have wit enough to distinguish truth from falsehood. And as I see no character in life more great or valuable than to be truly devout, nor anything more noble, or more beautiful, than the fervour of a sincere piety, so I think nothing more abominable than the outside daubing of a pretended zeal, than those mountebanks, those devotees in show, whose sacrilegious and treacherous grimace deceives with impunity, and according as they please, make a jest of what is most venerable and sacred among men. Those slaves of interest who make a trade of godliness, and who would purchase honours and reputation with a hypocritical turning up of the eyes and affected transports. Those people, I say, who show an uncommon zeal for the next world in order to make their fortunes in this, who, with great affectation and earnestness, daily recommend solitude, while they live in courts. Men who know how to make their own vices consistent with their zeal; they are passionate, revengeful, faithless, full of artifice; and to effect a man's destruction, they insolently urge their private resentment as the cause of Heaven; being so much the more dangerous in their wrath as they point against us those weapons which men reverence, and because their passions prompt them to assassinate us with a consecrated blade. There are too many of this vile character, but the sincerely devout are easily known; our age, brother, affords us some of these who might serve for glorious patterns to us. Observe Aristo, Periander, Orontes, Alcidamas, Polidore, Clitander; that title is refused to them by nobody. These are not braggadocios in virtue. We see none of this insufferable haughtiness in their conduct, and their devotion is humane and gentle. They censure not all we do, they think there's too much pride in these corrections, and leaving the fierceness of words to others, reprove our actions by their own. They never build upon the appearance of a fault, and are always ready to judge favourably of others. They have no cabals, no intrigues to carry on; their chief aim is to live themselves as they should do. They never worry a poor sinner; their quarrel is only with the offence. Nor do they ever exert a keener zeal for the interest of Heaven than Heaven itself does. These are the men for me; this is the true practice, and this the example fit to be followed. Your man is indeed not of this stamp. You cry up his zeal out of a good intention, but I believe you are imposed on by a very false gloss.

ORGON.   My dear brother, have you done?

CLÉANTE.   Yes.

ORGON.   [*Going*] Then I'm your humble servant.

CLÉANTE.   Pray one word more, brother; let us leave this discourse. You know you promised to take Valère for your son-in-law.

ORGON.   Yes.

CLÉANTE.   And have appointed a day for this agreeable wedding.

ORGON.   True.

CLÉANTE.   Why then do you put off the solemnity?

ORGON.   I can't tell.

CLÉANTE.   Have you some other design in your head?

ORGON.   Perhaps so.

CLÉANTE.   Will you break your word, then?

ORGON.   I don't say that.

CLÉANTE.   I think there's no obstacle can hinder you from performing your promise.

ORGON.   That's as it happens.

CLÉANTE.   Does the speaking of a single word require so much circumspection, then? Valère sends me to you about it.

ORGON.   Heaven be praised!

CLÉANTE.   What answer shall I return him?

ORGON.   What you will.

CLÉANTE.   But 'tis necessary I should know your intentions; pray what are they?

ORGON.   To do just what Heaven pleases.

CLÉANTE.   But to the point, pray. Valère has your promise; do you stand to it, ay or no?

ORGON.   Good be t'ye.

CLÉANTE.   [*Alone*] I am afraid he'll meet with some misfortune in his love. I ought to inform him how matters go.

Act II.

Scene I.

ORGON, MARIANE.

ORGON.   Mariane!

MARIANE.   Sir.

ORGON.   Come hither; I have something to say to you in private.

MARIANE.   [*To* ORGON, *who is looking into a closet*] What are you looking for, sir?

ORGON.   I'm looking if anybody's there who might overhear us. This little place is fit for such a purpose. So, we're all safe. I have always, Mariane, found you of a sweet disposition, and you have always been very dear to me.

MARIANE.   I am very much obliged to you, sir, for your fatherly affection.

ORGON.   'Tis very well said, daughter, and to deserve it, your chief care should be to make me easy.

MARIANE.   That is the height of my ambition.

ORGON.   Very well. Then what say you of Tartuffe, our guest?

MARIANE.   Who, I?

ORGON.   Yes, you; pray take heed how you answer.

MARIANE.   Alas! sir, I'll say what you will of him.

Scene II.

ORGON, MARIANE, DORINE, *who comes in softly, and stands behind* ORGON *without being seen.*

ORGON.   That's discreetly said. Tell me then, my girl, that he's a very deserving person, that you like him, and that it would be agreeable if, with my consent, you might have him for a husband, ha?

MARIANE.   How, sir?

ORGON.   What's the matter?

MARIANE.   What said you?

ORGON.   What?

MARIANE.   Did I mistake you?

ORGON.   As how?

MARIANE.   Whom would you have me say I liked, sir, and should be glad, with your approbation, to have for a husband?

ORGON.   Tartuffe.

MARIANE.   I protest to you, sir, there's nothing in it. Why would you make me tell you such a story?

ORGON.   But I would have it to be no story, and 'tis enough that I have pitched upon him for you.

MARIANE.   What, would you, sir—

ORGON.   Ay, child, I purpose, by your marriage, to join Tartuffe to my family. I have resolved upon't, and as I have a right to— [*Spying* DORINE] What business have you there? Your curiosity is very great, sweetheart, to bring you to listen in this manner.

DORINE.   In troth, sir, whether this report proceeds from conjecture or chance, I don't know; but they have been just telling me the news of this match, and I have been making a very great jest of it.

ORGON.   Why, is the thing so incredible?

DORINE.   So incredible that were you to tell me so yourself, I should not believe you.

ORGON.   I know how to make you believe it, though.

DORINE.   Ay, ay, sir, you tell us a comical story.

ORGON.   I tell you just what will prove true in a short time.

DORINE.   Stuff!

ORGON.   [*To* MARIANE] Daughter, I promise you I'm not in jest.

DORINE.   Go, go; don't believe your father, madame, he does but joke.

ORGON.   I tell you—

DORINE.   No, 'tis in vain, nobody will believe you.

ORGON.   My anger at length—

DORINE.   Well, sir, we will believe you; and so much the worse on your side. What, sir, is it possible that with that air of wisdom, and that spacious beard on your face, you should be weak enough but to wish—

ORGON.   Harkee, you have taken certain liberties of late that I dislike. I tell you that, child.

DORINE.   Good sir, let us argue this affair calmly. You really must banter people by this scheme. Your daughter is not cut out for a bigot; he has other things to think on. And then, what will such an alliance bring you in? For what reason would you go, with all your wealth, to choose a beggar for a son-in-law—

ORGON.   Hold your tongue! If he has nothing, know that we ought to esteem him for it. His poverty is an honest poverty which raises him above all grandeur, because he has suffered himself, in short, to be deprived of his fortune by his negligence for things temporal and his strong attachment to things eternal. But my assistance may put him in a way of getting out of trouble and of recovering his own. As poor as he is, he's a gentleman, and the estate he was born to is not inconsiderable.

DORINE.   Yes, he says so; and this vanity, sir, does not very well suit with piety. He that embraces the simplicity of a holy life should not set forth his name and family so much. The humble procedure of devotion does but ill agree with the glare of ambition. To what purpose all this pride?—But this talk offends you. Then let us lay aside his quality, and speak to his person. Can you have the heart to fling away such a girl as this upon such a man as he? Should you not consult propriety, and look a little forward to the consequences of such a union as this? Depend upon't, a young woman's virtue is in some danger when she isn't married to her mind; that her living virtuously afterward depends, in a great measure, upon the good qualities of her husband; and that those whom people everywhere point at with the finger to the forehead, often make their wives what we find they are. It is no easy task to be faithful to some sorts of husbands; and he that gives his daughter a man she hates, is accountable to Heaven for the slips she makes. Consider then to what danger your design exposes you.

ORGON.   I tell you, she is to learn from me what to do.

DORINE.   You could not do better with her than to follow my advice.

ORGON.   Don't let us amuse ourselves, daughter, with this silly stuff. I am your father, and know what you must do. I had indeed promised you to Valère, but, besides that 'tis reported he is given to play, I suspect him of being a little profligate. I don't observe that he frequents the church.

DORINE.   Would you have him run to church at your precise hours, as people do who go there only to be taken notice of?

ORGON.   I am not consulting you about it. [*To his daughter*] The other, in short, is a favourite of Heaven, and that is beyond any other possessions. This union will crown your wishes with every sort of good; it will be one continued scene of pleasure and delight. You'll live in faithful love together, really like two children, like two turtle-doves. No unhappy debate will e'er rise between you; and you'll make anything of him you can well desire.

DORINE.   She? She'll ne'er make anything but a fool of him, I assure you.

ORGON.   Hey! What language!

DORINE.   I say, he has the look of a fool; and his ascendant will overbear all the virtue your daughter has.

ORGON.   Have done with your interruptions. Learn to hold your peace, and don't you put in your oar where you have nothing to do.

DORINE.   Nay, sir, I only speak for your good.

ORGON.   You are too officious. Pray hold your tongue, if you please.

DORINE.   If one had not a love for you—

ORGON.   I desire none of your love.

DORINE.   But I will love you, sir, in spite of your teeth.

ORGON.   Ha!

DORINE.   I have your reputation much at heart, and can't bear to have you made the subject of every gossip's tale.

ORGON.   Then you won't have done?

DORINE.   It would be a sin to let you make such an alliance as this.

ORGON.   Will you hold your tongue, you serpent, whose impudence—

DORINE.   Oh! what, a devotee, and fly into such a rage?

ORGON.   Yes, my choler is moved at this impertinence, and I'm resolved you shall hold your tongue.

DORINE.   Be it so. But though I don't speak a word, I don't think the less.

ORGON.   Think if you will, but take care not to say a syllable to me about it, or—Enough—[*To his daughter*] I have maturely weighed all things as a wise man should.

DORINE.   [*Aside*] It makes me mad that I must not speak now!

ORGON.   Tartuffe, without foppery, is a person so formed—

DORINE.   [*Aside*] Yes, 'tis a pretty phiz.

ORGON.   That should you have no great relish for his other qualifications—

DORINE.   [*Aside*] She'll have a very fine bargain of him! [ORGON *turns about towards* DORINE, *and eyes her with his arms across.*] Were I in her place, though, no man alive should marry me against my will, with impunity. I'd let him see, soon after the ceremony was over, that a wife has a revenge always at hand.

ORGON.   [*To* DORINE] Then what I say, stands for nothing with you?

DORINE.   What do you complain of? I don't speak to you.

ORGON.   What is it you do then?

DORINE.   I talk to myself.

ORGON.   [*Aside*] Very well! I must give her a slap on the face, to correct her prodigious insolence. [*He puts himself into a posture to strike* DORINE, *and at every word he speaks to his daughter he casts his eyes upon* DORINE, *who stands bolt-upright, without speaking.*] Daughter, you must needs approve of my design—and believe that the husband—which I have picked out for you—[*To* DORINE] Why dost thou not talk to thyself now?

DORINE.   Because I have nothing to say to myself.

ORGON.   One little word more.

DORINE.   I've no mind to it.

ORGON.   To be sure I watched you.

DORINE.   A downright fool, i'faith.

ORGON.   [*To* MARIANE] In short, daughter, you must obey, and show an entire deference for my choice.

DORINE.   [*As she runs off*] I should scorn to take such a husband myself.

ORGON.   [*Strikes at her, but misses*] You have a pestilent hussy with you there, daughter, that I can't live with any longer, without sin. I'm not in a condition to proceed at present; her insolence has put my spirits into such a ferment that I must go take the air to recover myself a little.

Scene III.

MARIANE, DORINE.

DORINE.   Pray tell me, have you lost your tongue? Must I play your part for you on this occasion? What, suffer a silly overture to be made you, without saying the least word against it!

MARIANE.   What should one do with a positive father?

DORINE.   Anything, to ward off such a menace.

MARIANE.   But what?

DORINE.   Why, tell him that hearts admit of no proxies; that you marry for yourself, and not for him; that you being the person for whom the whole affair is transacted, your inclinations for the man should be consulted, not his; and that if Tartuffe seems so lovely in his eyes, he may marry him himself without let or hindrance.

MARIANE.   A father, I own, has such a command over one that I never had courage to make him a reply.

DORINE.   But let us reason the case. Valère has made advances for you; pray, do you love him, or do you not?

MARIANE.   Nay, you do injustice to my love, to question my affections! Ought you, Dorine, to ask me that? Have I not opened my heart to you a hundred times on that subject? and are you still a stranger to the warmth of my passion?

DORINE.   How do I know whether your heart and words keep pace together? or whether you really have any particular regard for this lover or not?

MARIANE.   You do me wrong, Dorine, to doubt it; and the sincerity of my sentiments, in that matter, has been but too plain.

DORINE.   You really love him, then?

MARIANE.   Ay, extremely.

DORINE.   And according to all appearance, he loves you as well.

MARIANE.   I believe so.

DORINE.   And you two have a mutual desire to marry?

MARIANE.   Assuredly.

DORINE.   What is then your expectation from this other match?

MARIANE.   To kill myself, if they force me to it.

DORINE.   Very good! That's a relief I did not think of; you need only to die to get rid of this perplexity. 'Tis a wonderful remedy, for certain. It makes one mad to hear folks talk at this rate.

MARIANE.   Bless me, Dorine! what a humour are you got into! You have no compassion upon people's afflictions.

DORINE.   I have no compassion for people who talk idly and give way in time of action as you do.

MARIANE.   But what would you have, if one is timorous?

DORINE.   But love requires a firmness of mind.

MARIANE.   But have I wavered in my affections towards Valère? And is it not his business to gain me of my father?

DORINE.   But what? if your father be a downright humorist, who is entirely bewitched with his Tartuffe, and would set aside a match he had agreed on, pray is that your lover's fault?

MARIANE.   But should I, by a flat and confident refusal, let everybody know that I am violently in love? Would you have me, for his sake, transgress the modesty of my sex and the bounds of my duty? Would you have my passion become a perfect town-talk?

DORINE.   No, no, I don't want anything. I see you'd fain have Monsieur Tartuffe; and now I think of it, I should be in the wrong to dissuade you from so considerable an alliance. To what purpose should I oppose your inclinations? The match is in itself too advantageous. Monsieur Tartuffe, oh! is this a trifling offer? If we take it right, he's no simpleton. It will be no small honour to be his mate. All the world has a prodigious value for him already; he is well born, handsome in his person, he has a red ear, and a very florid complexion; you'll, in short, be but too happy with such a husband.

MARIANE.   Heavens!

DORINE.   You can't conceive what a joy 'twill be to you to be the consort of so fine a man!

MARIANE.   Poh! prithee give over this discourse, and rather assist me against this match. 'Tis now all over; I yield, and am ready to do whatever you'd have me.

DORINE.   No, no, a daughter should do as she's bid, though her father would have her marry a monkey. Besides, what reason have you to complain? Yours is a benefit ticket. You'll be coached down to his own borough-town, which you'll find abounds in cousins and uncles. It will be very diverting to you to entertain them all. Then Madame Tartuffe will be directly introduced to the beau-monde. You'll go visit, by way of welcome, the bailiff's lady and the assessor's wife; they'll do you the honour of the folding chair. At a good time you may hope for a ball, and a great consort, to wit, two pair of bagpipes; and perchance you may see merry-Andrew and the puppet-show; if, however, your husband—

MARIANE.   Oh! you kill me! Rather contrive how to help me by your advice.

DORINE.   Your humble servant for that.

MARIANE.   Nay, Dorine, for Heaven's sake—

DORINE.   No, it must be a match, to punish you.

MARIANE.   Dear girl, do!

DORINE.   No.

MARIANE.   If my professions—

DORINE.   No, Tartuffe's your man, and you shall have a taste of him.

MARIANE.   You know how much I always confided in you; be so good—

DORINE.   No, in troth; you shall be Tartuffed.

MARIANE.   Well, since my misfortunes can't move you, henceforth leave me entirely to my despair. That shall lend my heart relief, and I know an infallible remedy for all my sufferings. [*Offers to go*]

DORINE.   Here, here, come back; I'm appeased. I must take compassion on you, for all this.

MARIANE.   I tell you, d'y' see, Dorine, if they do expose me to this torment, it will certainly cost me my life.

DORINE.   Don't vex yourself, it may easily be prevented—But see, here's your humble servant Valère.

Scene IV.

VALÈRE, MARIANE, DORINE.

VALÈRE.   I was just now told an odd piece of news, madame, that I knew nothing of, and which to be sure is very pretty.

MARIANE.   What's that?

VALÈRE.   That you are to be married to Tartuffe.

MARIANE.　'Tis certain my father has such a design in his head.

VALÈRE.　Your father, madame—

MARIANE.　Has altered his mind, and has been just now making the proposal to me.

VALÈRE.　What, seriously?

MARIANE.　Ay, seriously. He has been declaring himself strenuously for the match.

VALÈRE.　And pray, madame, what may be your determination in the affair?

MARIANE.　I don't know.

VALÈRE.　The answer is honest! You don't know?

MARIANE.　No.

VALÈRE.　No?

MARIANE.　What would you advise me to?

VALÈRE.　I advise you to accept of him for a husband.

MARIANE.　Is that your advice?

VALÈRE.　Yes.

MARIANE.　In good earnest?

VALÈRE.　No doubt of it. The choice is good, and well worth attending to.

MARIANE.　Well, sir, I shall take your counsel.

VALÈRE.　You will have no difficulty to follow it, I believe.

MARIANE.　Hardly more than your counsel gave you.

VALÈRE.　I gave it, madame, to please you.

MARIANE.　And I shall follow it, to do you a pleasure.

DORINE.　[*Retiring to the farther part of the stage*] So. Let's see what this will come to.

VALÈRE.　Is this, then, your affection? And was it all deceit, when you—

MARIANE.　Pray let's talk no more of that. You told me frankly that I ought to accept of the offer made me. And I tell you, I shall do so, only because you advise me to it as the best.

VALÈRE.　Don't excuse yourself upon my intentions. Your resolution was made before, and you now lay hold of a frivolous pretence for the breaking of your word.

MARIANE.　'Tis true; it's well said.

VALÈRE.　Doubtless, and you never had any true love for me.

MARIANE.　Alas! You may think so if you please.

VALÈRE.　Yes, yes, may think so; but my offended heart may chance to be beforehand with you in that affair, and I can tell where to offer both my addresses and my hand.

MARIANE.　I don't doubt it, sir. The warmth that merit raises—

VALÈRE.　Lack-a-day! Let us drop merit. I have little enough of that, and you think so; but I hope another will treat me in a kinder manner; and I know a person whose heart, open to my retreat, will not be ashamed to make up my loss.

MARIANE.   The loss is not great, and you will be comforted upon this change easily enough.

VALÈRE.   You may believe I shall do all that lies in my power. A heart that forgets us, engages our glory; we must employ our utmost cares to forget it too; and if we don't succeed, we must at least pretend we do; for to show a regard for those that forsake us, is a meanness one cannot answer to one's self.

MARIANE.   The sentiment is certainly noble and sublime.

VALÈRE.   Very well, and what everybody must approve of. What? would you have me languish for ever for you? See you fly into another's arms before my face, and not transfer my slighted affections somewhere else?

MARIANE.   So far from that, 'tis what I would have; and I wish 'twere done already.

VALÈRE.   You wish it done?

MARIANE.   Yes.

VALÈRE.   That's insulting me sufficiently, madame; I am just going to give you that satisfaction. [*He offers to go*]

MARIANE.   'Tis very well.

VALÈRE.   [*Returning*] Be pleased to remember, at least, that 'tis yourself who drive me to this extremity.

MARIANE.   Yes.

VALÈRE.   [*Returning again*] And that the design I have conceived is only from your example.

MARIANE.   My example be it.

VALÈRE.   [*Going*] Enough, you shall soon be punctually obeyed.

MARIANE.   So much the better.

VALÈRE.   [*Returning again*] 'Tis the last time I shall ever trouble you.

MARIANE.   With all my heart.

VALÈRE.   [*Goes toward the door and returns*] Hey?

MARIANE.   What's the matter?

VALÈRE.   Didn't you call me?

MARIANE.   Who, I? You dream, sure.

VALÈRE.   Well, then, I'll be gone; farewell, madame!

MARIANE.   Fare ye well, sir.

DORINE.   [*To* MARIANE] I think, for my part, by this piece of extravagance, you've both lost your senses. I have let you alone thus long squabbling, to see what end you'd make of it. Hark ye, Monsieur Valère! [*She lays hold of* VALÈRE's *arm*]

VALÈRE. [*Pretending to resist*] Hey! What would you have, Dorine?

DORINE. Come hither.

VALÈRE. No, no, my indignation overpowers me; don't hinder me from doing as she would have me.

DORINE. Stay.

VALÈRE. No, d'ye see, I'm resolved upon it.

DORINE. Ah!

MARIANE. [*Aside*] He's uneasy at the sight of me. My presence drives him away; I had much better therefore leave the place.

DORINE. [*Quitting* VALÈRE, *and running after* MARIANE] What, t'other? whither do you run?

MARIANE. Let me alone.

DORINE. You must come back.

MARIANE. No, no, Dorine; in vain you'd hold me.

VALÈRE. [*Aside*] I find that my presence is but a plague to her. I had certainly better free her from it.

DORINE. [*Quitting* MARIANE, *and running after* VALÈRE] What, again? Deuce take you for me. Leave this fooling, and come hither both of you. [*She takes* VALÈRE *and* MARIANE *by the hand, and brings them back*]

VALÈRE. But what's your design?

MARIANE. What would you do?

DORINE. Set you two to rights again, and bring you out of this scrape. [*To* VALÈRE] Aren't you mad, to wrangle at this rate?

VALÈRE. Didn't you hear how she spoke to me?

DORINE. [*To* MARIANE] Weren't you a simpleton, to be in such a passion?

MARIANE. Didn't you see the thing, and how he treated me?

DORINE. Folly on both sides. [*To* VALÈRE] She has nothing more at heart than that she may be one day yours; I am witness to it. [*To* MARIANE] He loves none but yourself, and has no other ambition than to become your husband, I answer for it upon my life.

MARIANE. [*To* VALÈRE] Why then did you give me such advice?

VALÈRE. [*To* MARIANE] And why was I consulted upon such a subject?

DORINE. You're a couple of fools. Come, come, your hands, both of you; [*To* VALÈRE] come, you.

VALÈRE. [*Giving his hand to* DORINE] What will my hand do?

DORINE. [*To* MARIANE] So; come, now yours.

MARIANE. [*Giving her hand*] To what purpose is all this?

DORINE. Come along, come quick: you love one another better than you think of.

VALÈRE.   [*Turning toward* MARIANE] But don't do things with an ill grace, and give a body a civil look.

[MARIANE *turns toward* VALÈRE, *and smiles a little*]

DORINE.   In troth, lovers are silly creatures!

VALÈRE.   [*To* MARIANE] Now, have I not room to complain of you; and, without lying, were not you a wicked creature, to gratify yourself in saying a thing so very shocking to me?

MARIANE.   But are not you the ungratefullest man in the world—

DORINE.   Come let's adjourn this debate till another time; and think how to ward off this plaguy wedding.

MARIANE.   Say, then, what engines shall we set at work?

DORINE.   We'll set them every way to work. [*To* MARIANE] Your father's in jest; [*To* VALÈRE] it must be nothing but talk. [*To* MARIANE] But for your part, your best way will be to carry the appearance of a gentle compliance with his extravagance, that so, in case of an alarm, you may have it more easily in your power to delay the marriage proposed. In gaining time we shall remedy everything. Sometimes you may fob 'em off with some illness, which is to come all of a sudden and will require delay. Sometimes you may fob 'em off with ill omens. You unluckily met a corpse, broke a looking-glass, or dreamed dirty water; and at last, the best on't is, they can't possibly join you to any other but him, unless you please to say, Yes. But, the better to carry on the design, I think it proper you should not be seen conferring together. [*To* VALÈRE] Go you immediately and employ your friends, that he may be forced to keep his word with you. [*To* MARIANE] Let us go excite his brother's endeavours, and engage the mother-in-law in our party. Adieu.

VALÈRE.   [*To* MARIANE] Whatever efforts any of us may be preparing, my greatest hope, to say the truth, is in you.

MARIANE.   [*To* VALÈRE] I can't promise for the inclinations of a father, but I shall be none but Valère's.

VALÈRE.   How you transport me! And though I durst—

DORINE.   Ah! These lovers are never weary of prattling. Away, I tell you.

VALÈRE.   [*Goes a step or two, and returns*] Once more—

DORINE.   What a clack is yours! Draw you off this way, and you t'other. [*Pushing them each out by the shoulders*]

Act III.

Scene I.

DAMIS, DORINE.

DAMIS.   May thunder, this moment, strike me dead; let me be everywhere treated like the greatest scoundrel alive, if any respect or power whatever shall stop me, and if I don't strike some masterly stroke.

DORINE.   Moderate your passion for Heaven's sake; your father did but barely mention it. People don't do all they propose, and the distance is great from the project to the execution.

DAMIS.   I must put a stop to this fool's projects, and tell him a word or two in his ear.

DORINE.   Gently, gently, pray; let your mother-in-law alone with him, as well as with your father. She has some credit with Tartuffe. He is mighty complaisant to all she says, and perhaps he may have a sneaking kindness for her. I would to Heaven it were true! That would be charming. In short, your interest obliges her to send for him; she has a mind to sound his intentions with regard to the wedding that disturbs you, and represent to him the fatal feuds he will raise in the family if he entertains any hopes of this affair. His man says that he's at prayers, and I could not see him. But this servant told me he would not be long before he came down. Then pray be gone, and let me stay for him.

DAMIS.   I may be present at this whole conference.

DORINE.   No, they must be by themselves.

DAMIS.   I shall say nothing to him.

DORINE.   You're mistaken; we know the usual impatience of your temper, and 'tis the ready way to spoil all. Get away.

DAMIS.   No, I will see him without putting myself in a passion.

DORINE.   How troublesome you are! He's coming; retire. [DAMIS *conceals himself in a closet*]

Scene II.

TARTUFF, DORINE.

TARTUFFE.   [*Upon seeing* DORINE *speaks aloud to his servant who is in the house*] Laurence, lock up my hair-cloth and scourge, and beg of Heaven ever to enlighten you with grace. If anybody comes to see me, I am gone to the prisons to distribute my alms.

DORINE.   [*Aside*] What affectation and roguery!

TARTUFFE.   What do you want?

DORINE.   To tell you—

TARTUFFE.   [*Drawing a handkerchief out of his pocket*] Oh! lack-a-day pray take me this handkerchief before you speak.

DORINE.   What for?

TARTUFFE.   Cover that bosom, which I can't bear to see. Such objects hurt the soul, and usher in sinful thoughts.

DORINE.   You mightily melt then at a temptation, and the flesh makes great impression upon your senses? Truly, I can't tell what heat may inflame you; but, for my part, I am not so apt to hanker. Now I could see you stark naked from head to foot, and that whole hide of yours not tempt me at all.

TARTUFFE.   Pray, now, speak with a little modesty, or I shall leave you this minute.

DORINE.   No, no, 'tis I who am going to leave you to yourself; and I have only two words to say to you: My lady is coming down into this parlour, and desires the favour of a word with you.

TARTUFFE.   Alack! with all my heart.

DORINE.   [*Aside*] How sweet he grows upon it! I'faith, I still stand to what I said of him.

TARTUFFE.   Will she come presently?

DORINE.   I think I hear her. Ay, 'tis she herself; I leave you together.

Scene III.

ELMIRE, TARTUFFE.

TARTUFFE.   May Heaven, of its goodness, ever bestow upon you health both of body and of mind! and bless your days equal to the wish of the lowest of its votaries!

ELMIRE.   I am much obliged to you for this pious wish; but let us take a seat to be more at ease.

TARTUFFE.   [*Sitting down*] Do you find your indisposition anything bated?

ELMIRE. [*Sitting*] Very well; my fever soon left me.

TARTUFFE. My prayers have not sufficient merit to have drawn down this favour from above, but I made no vows to Heaven that did not concern your recovery.

ELMIRE. Your zeal for me was too solicitous.

TARTUFFE. Your dear health cannot be overrated; and, to re-establish it, I could have sacrificed my own.

ELMIRE. That is carrying Christian charity a great way, and I am highly indebted to you for all this goodness.

TARTUFFE. I do much less for you than you deserve.

ELMIRE. I had a desire to speak with you in private on a certain affair, and am glad that nobody observes us here.

TARTUFFE. I am also overjoyed at it; and, be sure, it can be no ordinary satisfaction, madame, to find myself alone with you. 'Tis an opportunity that I have hitherto petitioned Heaven for in vain.

ELMIRE. What I want to talk with you upon is a small matter in which your whole heart must be open and hide nothing from me.

TARTUFFE. And, for this singular favour, I certainly will unbosom myself to you without the least reserve; and I protest to you that the stir I made about the visits paid here to your charms, was not out of hatred to you, but rather out of a passionate zeal which induced me to it, and out of a pure motive—

ELMIRE. For my part I take it very well, and believe 'tis my good that gives you this concern.

TARTUFFE. [*Taking* ELMIRE's *hand, and squeezing her fingers*] Yes, madame, without doubt, and such is the fervour of my—

ELMIRE. Oh! you squeeze me too hard.

TARTUFFE. 'Tis out of excess of zeal; I never intended to hurt you. I had much rather—[*Puts his hand upon her knee*]

ELMIRE. What does your hand do there?

TARTUFFE. I'm only feeling your clothes, madame; the stuff is mighty rich.

ELMIRE. Oh! Pray give over; I am very ticklish. [*She draws away her chair, and* TARTUFFE *follows with his*]

TARTUFFE. Bless me! How wonderful is the workmanship of this lace! They work to a miracle nowadays. Things of all kinds were never better done.

ELMIRE. 'Tis true; but let us speak to our affair a little. They say that my husband has a mind to set aside his promise, and to give you his daughter. Is that true? Pray tell me.

TARTUFFE. He did hint something towards it. But, madame, to tell you the truth, that is not the happiness I sigh after. I behold elsewhere the wonderful attractions of the felicity that engages every wish of mine.

ELMIRE.   That is, you love no earthly things.

TARTUFFE.   My breast does not enclose a heart of flint.

ELMIRE.   I am apt to think that your sighs tend all to Heaven, and that nothing here below can detain your desires.

TARTUFFE.   The love which engages us to eternal beauties does not extinguish in us the love of temporal ones. Our senses may easily be charmed with the perfect works Heaven has formed. Its reflected charms shine forth in such as you. But in your person it displays its choicest wonders. It has diffused such beauties o'er your face as surprise the sight and transport the heart; nor could I behold you, perfect creature, without admiring in you the Author of nature, and feeling my heart touched with an ardent love at sight of the fairest of portraits wherein he has delineated himself. At first I was under apprehensions lest this secret flame might be a dexterous surprise of the foul fiend; and my heart even resolved to avoid your eyes, believing you an obstacle to my future happiness. But at length I perceived, most lovely beauty, that my passion could not be blameable, that I could reconcile it with modesty, and this made me abandon my heart to it. It is, I confess, a very great presumption in me to make you the offer of this heart; but, in my vows, I rely wholly on your goodness, and not on anything in my own weak power. In you centre my hope, my happiness, my quiet; on you depend my torment or my bliss; and I am on the point of being, by your sole decision, happy if you will, or miserable if you please.

ELMIRE.   The declaration is extremely gallant, but, to say the truth, it is a good deal surprising. Methinks you ought to have fortified your mind better, and to have reasoned a little upon a design of this nature. A devotee as you are, whom every one speaks of as—

TARTUFFE.   Ah! being a devotee does not make me the less a man; and when one comes to view your celestial charms, the heart surrenders, and reasons no more. I know that such language from me seems somewhat strange; but, madame, after all, I am not an angel, and should you condemn the declaration I make, you must lay the blame upon your attractive charms. From the moment I first set eyes upon your more than human splendour, you became the sovereign of my soul. The ineffable sweetness of your divine looks broke through the resistance which my heart obstinately made. It surmounted everything, fastings, prayers, tears, and turned all my vows on the side of your charms. My eyes and my sighs have told it you a thousand times, and the better to explain myself I here make use of words. Now if you contemplate with some benignity of soul the tribulations of your unworthy slave; if your goodness will give me consolation, and deign to debase itself so low as my nothingness, I shall ever entertain for you, miracle of sweetness, a devotion which nothing can equal. Your honour, with me, runs no risk, it need fear no disgrace on my part. All those courtly gallants the ladies are so fond of, make a bustle in what they do, and are vain in what they say. We see they are ever vaunting of their success; they receive no favours that they don't divulge, and their indiscreet tongues, which people confide in, dishonour the altar on which their hearts offer sacrifice. But men of our sort burn with a discreet flame, with whom a secret is always sure to remain such. The care we take of our own reputation is an undeniable security to the persons beloved. And 'tis with us, when they accept our hearts, that they enjoy love without scandal and pleasure without fear.

ELMIRE.   I hear what you say, and your rhetoric explains itself to me in terms sufficiently strong. Don't you apprehend that I may take a fancy now to acquaint my husband with this gallantry of yours? and that an early account of an amour of this sort might pretty much alter his present affections towards you?

TARTUFFE.   I know that you are too good, and that you will rather pardon my temerity; that you will excuse me, upon the score of human frailty, the sallies of a passion that offends you; and will consider, when you consult your glass, that a man is not blind, and is made of flesh and blood.

ELMIRE.   Some might take it perhaps in another manner; but I shall show my discretion, and not tell my husband of it. But in return I will have one thing of you, that is honestly and sincerely to forward the match between Valère and Mariane, and that you yourself renounce the unjust power whereby you hope to be enriched with what belongs to another. And—

Scene IV.

ELMIRE, DAMIS, TARTUFFE.

DAMIS.   [*Coming out of the closet where he was hidden*] No, madame, no, this ought to be made public. I was in this place and overheard it all; and the goodness of Heaven seems to have directed me thither to confound the pride of a traitor that wrongs me, to open me a way to take vengeance of his hypocrisy and insolence, to undeceive my father and show him, in a clear light, the soul of a villain that talks to you of love.

ELMIRE.   No, Damis, 'tis enough that he reforms and endeavours to deserve the favour I do him. Since I have promised him, don't make me break my word. 'Tis not my humour to make a noise; a wife will make herself merry with such follies and never trouble her husband's ears with them.

DAMIS.   You have your reasons for using him in that manner, and I have mine too for acting otherwise. To spare him would be ridiculous; the insolent pride of his bigotry has triumphed too much over my just resentment, and created too many disorders among us already. The rascal has but too long governed my father and opposed my passion, as well as Valère's. 'Tis fit the perfidious wretch should be laid open to him, and Heaven for this purpose offers me an easy way to do it. I am greatly indebted to it for the opportunity; it is too favourable a one to be neglected, and I should deserve to have it taken from me now I have it, should I not make use of it.

ELMIRE.   Damis—

DAMIS.   No, by your leave, I must take my own counsel. My heart overflows with joy, and all you can say would in vain dissuade me from the pleasure of avenging myself. Without going any farther, I will make an end of the affair, and here's just what will give me satisfaction.

Scene V.

ORGON, ELMIRE, DAMIS, TARTUFFE.

DAMIS.   We are going to entertain you, sir, with an adventure spick and span new, which will very much surprise you. You are well rewarded for all your caresses, and this gentleman makes a fine acknowledgment of your tenderness. His great zeal for you is just come to light; it aims at nothing less than the dishonour of your bed, and I took him here making an injurious declaration of a criminal love to your wife. She is good-natured, and her over-great discretion, by all means, would have kept the secret; but I can't encourage such impudence, and think that not to apprise you of it is to do you an injury.

ELMIRE.   Yes, I am of opinion that one ought never to break in upon a husband's rest with such idle stuff, that our honour can by no means depend upon it, and that 'tis enough we know how to defend ourselves. These are my thoughts of the matter; and you would have said nothing, Damis, if I had had any credit with you.

Scene VI.

ORGON, DAMIS, TARTUFFE.

ORGON.   Heavens! What have I heard? Is this credible?

TARTUFFE.   Yes, brother, I am a wicked, guilty, wretched sinner, full of iniquity, the greatest villain that ever breathed. Every instant of my life is crowded with stains; 'tis one continued series of crimes and defilements; and I see that Heaven, for my punishment, designs to mortify me on this occasion. Whatever great offence they can lay to my charge, I shall have more humility than to deny it. Believe what they tell you, arm your resentment, and like a criminal, drive me out of your house. I cannot have so great a share of shame but I have still deserved a much larger.

ORGON. [*To his son*] Ah, traitor! darest thou, by this falsehood, attempt to tarnish the purity of his virtue?

DAMIS. What! shall the feigned meekness of this hypocritical soul make you give the lie—

ORGON. Thou cursed plague! hold thy tongue.

TARTUFFE. Ah! let him speak; you chide him wrongfully; you had much better believe what he tells you. Why so favourable to me upon such a fact? Do you know after all what I may be capable of? Can you, my brother, depend upon my outside? Do you think me the better for what you see of me? No, no, you suffer yourself to be deceived by appearances, and I am neither better nor worse, alas! than these people think me. The world indeed takes me for a very good man, but the truth is, I am a very worthless creature. [*Turning to* DAMIS] Yes, my dear child, say on, call me treacherous, infamous, reprobate, thief, and murderer; load me with names still more detestable; I don't gainsay you; I have deserved them all, and am willing on my knees to suffer the ignominy, as a shame due to the enormities of my life.

ORGON. [*To* TARTUFFE] This is too much, brother. [*To his son*] Does not thy heart relent, traitor?

DAMIS. What, shall his words so far deceive you as to—

ORGON. Hold your tongue, rascal! [*Raising* TARTUFFE] For Heaven's sake, brother, rise. [*To his son*] Infamous wretch!

DAMIS. He can—

ORGON. Hold thy tongue.

DAMIS. Intolerable! What! am I taken for—

ORGON. Say one other word and I'll break thy bones.

TARTUFFE. For Heaven's sake, brother, don't be angry; I had rather suffer any hardship than that he should get the slightest hurt on my account.

ORGON. [*To his son*] Ungrateful monster!

TARTUFFE. Let him alone; if I must on my knees ask forgiveness for him—

ORGON. [*Throwing himself also at* TARTUFFE's *feet, and embracing him*] Alas! You are in jest, sure? [*To his son*] See his goodness, sirrah!

DAMIS. Then—

ORGON. Have done.

DAMIS. What! I—

ORGON.   Peace, I say. I know what put you upon this attack well
enough; ye all hate him, and I now see wife, children, servants, are all
let loose against him. They impudently try every way to remove this devout person from me. But the more they strive to get him out, the
greater care will I take to keep him in; and therefore will I hasten his
marriage with my daughter, to confound the pride of the whole family.

DAMIS.   Do you think to force her to accept of him?

ORGON.   Yes, traitor, and this very evening, to plague you. Nay, I
defy you all, and shall make you to know that I am master, and will be
obeyed. Come, sirrah, do you recant; immediately throw yourself at his
feet to beg his pardon.

DAMIS.   Who, I? of this rascal, who by his impostures—

ORGON.   What, scoundrel, do you rebel, and call him names? A
cudgel there, a cudgel. [*To* TARTUFFE] Don't hold me. [*To his son*] Get
you out of my house this minute, and never dare to set foot into it again.

DAMIS.   Yes, I shall go, but—

ORGON.   Quickly, then, leave the place; sirrah, I disinherit thee,
and give thee my curse besides.

Scene VII.

ORGON, TARTUFFE.

ORGON.   To offend a holy person in such a manner!

TARTUFFE.   [*Aside*] O Heaven! pardon him the anguish he gives
me! [*To* ORGON] Could you know what a grief it is to me that they
should try to blacken me with my dear brother—

ORGON.   Alack-a-day!

TARTUFFE.   The very thought of this ingratitude wounds me to the
very quick!—Lord, what horror!—My heart's so full that I can't speak;
I think I shan't outlive it.

ORGON.   [*Running all in tears to the door out of which he drove his
son*] Villain! I'm sorry my hand spared, and did not make an end of
thee on the spot. [*To* TARTUFFE] Compose yourself, brother, and don't
be troubled.

TARTUFFE.   Let us by all means put an end to the course of these
unhappy debates; I see what uneasiness I occasion here, and think
there's a necessity, brother, for my leaving your house.

ORGON.   How? You're not in earnest sure?

TARTUFFE.   They hate me, and seek, I see, to bring my integrity into
question with you.

ORGON.   What signifies that? Do you see me listen to them?

TARTUFFE.   They won't stop here, you may be sure; and those very stories which you now reject may one day meet with more credit.

ORGON.   No, brother, never.

TARTUFFE.   Ah! brother, a wife may easily deceive a husband.

ORGON.   No, no.

TARTUFFE.   Suffer me, by removing hence, immediately to remove from them all occasion of attacking me in this manner.

ORGON.   No, you must stay, or it will cost me my life.

TARTUFFE.   Well, then, I must mortify myself. If you would, however—

ORGON.   Ah!

TARTUFFE.   Be it so. Let's talk no more about it. But I know how I must behave on this occasion. Honour is delicate, and friendship obliges me to prevent reports and not to give any room for suspicion; I'll shun your wife, and you shall never see me—

ORGON.   No, in spite of everybody, you shall frequently be with her. To vex the world is my greatest joy, and I'll have you seen with her at all hours. This is not all yet, the better to brave them. I'll have no other heir but you, and I'm going forthwith to sign you a deed of gift for my whole estate. A true and hearty friend, that I fix on for a son-in-law, is far dearer to me than either son, wife, or kindred. You won't refuse what I propose?

TARTUFFE.   Heaven's will be done in all things.

ORGON.   Poor man! Come, let's get the writings drawn up, and then let envy burst itself with spite.

Act IV.

Scene I.
CLÉANTE, TARTUFFE.

CLÉANTE. Yes, 'tis in everybody's mouth, and you may believe me. The noise this rumour makes is not much to your credit; and I have met with you, sir, very opportunely, to tell you plainly, in two words, my thoughts of the matter. I shan't inquire into the ground of what's reported; I pass that by, and take the thing at worst. We'll suppose that Damis has not used you well, and that they have accused you wrongfully. Is it not the part of a good Christian to pardon the offence, and extinguish in his heart all desire of vengeance? Ought you to suffer a son to be turned out of his father's house on account of your differences? I tell you once again, and tell you frankly, there is neither small nor great but are scandalised at it. And if you take my advice, you'll make all up and not push matters to extremity. Sacrifice your resentment to your duty, and restore the son to his father's favour.

TARTUFFE. Alas! for my own part, I would do it with all my heart; I, sir, bear him not the least ill-will; I forgive him everything; I lay nothing to his charge, and would serve him with all my soul. But the interests of Heaven cannot admit of it: and if he comes in here again, I must go out. After such an unparalleled action, it would be scandalous for me to have anything to do with him. Heaven knows what all the world would immediately think on't. They would impute it to pure policy in me, and people would everywhere say that knowing myself guilty, I pretended a charitable zeal for my accuser; that I dreaded him at heart, and would practise upon him, that I might, underhand, engage him to silence.

CLÉANTE. You put us off here with sham excuses, and all your reasons, sir, are too far fetched. Why do you take upon you the interests of Heaven? Has it any occasion for our assistance in punishing the guilty?

33

Leave, leave the care of its own vengeance to itself, and only think of that pardon of offences which it prescribes; have no regard to the judgment of men when you follow the sovereign orders of Heaven! What! shall the paltry interest of what people may believe, hinder the glory of a good action! No, no, let us always do what Heaven has prescribed, and perplex our heads with no other care.

TARTUFFE. I have told you already that I forgive him from my heart, and that is doing, sir, what Heaven ordains; but after the scandal and affront of to-day, Heaven does not require me to live with him.

CLÉANTE. And does it require you, sir, to lend an ear to what mere caprice dictates to the father? And to accept of an estate where justice obliges you to make no pretensions?

TARTUFFE. Those that know me will never have the thought that this is the effect of an interested spirit. All the riches of this world have few charms for me; I am not dazzled by their false glare, and if I should resolve to accept this present, which the father has a mind to make me, it is, to tell you the truth, only because I'm afraid this means will fall into wicked hands, lest it should come amongst such as will make an ill use on't in the world, and not lay it out, as I intend to do, for the glory of Heaven and the good of my neighbour.

CLÉANTE. Oh, entertain none of these very nice scruples, which may occasion the complaints of a right heir. Let him, without giving yourself any trouble, keep his estate at his own peril, and consider that 'twere better he misused it than that people should accuse you for depriving him of it. I only wonder, that you could receive such a proposal without confusion. For, in short, has true zeal any maxim which shows how to strip a lawful heir of his right? And if it must be that Heaven has put into your heart an invincible obstacle to living with Damis, would it not be better, like a man of prudence, that you should fairly retire from hence than thus to suffer the eldest son, contrary to all reason, to be turned out of doors for you? Believe me, sir, this would give your discretion—

TARTUFFE. It is half an hour past three, sir. Certain devotions call me above stairs, and you'll excuse my leaving you so soon.

CLÉANTE. [*Alone*] Ah!

Scene II.

ELMIRE, MARIANE, CLÉANTE, DORINE.

DORINE. [*To* CLÉANTE] For goodness' sake, lend her what assistance you can, as we do. She's in the greatest perplexity, sir, imaginable; the articles her father has concluded for to-night make her every moment ready to despair. He's just a-coming; pray let us set on him in a body and try, either by force or cunning, to frustrate the unlucky design that has put us all into this consternation.

Scene III.

ORGON, ELMIRE, MARIANE, CLÉANTE, DORINE.

ORGON. Hah! I'm glad to see you all together. [*To* MARIANE] I bring something in this contract that will make you smile; you already know what this means.

MARIANE. [*Kneeling to* ORGON] Oh! sir, in the name of Heaven that is a witness of my grief, by everything that can move your heart, forgo a little the right nature has given you and dispense with my obedience in this particular. Don't compel me, by this hard law, to complain to Heaven of the duty I owe you. Do not, my father, render the life which you have given me unfortunate. If, contrary to the tender hopes I might have formed to myself, you won't suffer me to be the man's I presumed to love, at least, out of your goodness, which upon my knees I implore, save me from the torment of being the man's I abhor, and drive me not to despair by exerting your full power over me.

ORGON. [*Aside*] Come, stand firm, my heart; no human weakness.

MARIANE. Your tenderness for him gives me no uneasiness. Show it in the strongest manner, give him your estate; and if that's not enough, add all mine to it; I consent with all my heart, and give it up; but at least go not so far as to my person. Suffer a convent, with its austerities, to wear out the mournful days allotted me by Heaven.

ORGON. Ay, these are exactly your she-devotees, when a father crosses their wanton inclinations. Get up, get up; the more it goes against you, the more you'll merit by it. Mortify your senses by this marriage, and don't din me in the head any more about it.

DORINE. But what—

ORGON. Hold your tongue; speak to your own concerns. I absolutely forbid you to open your lips.

CLÉANTE. If you would indulge me, in answer, to give one word of advice.

ORGON. Brother, your advice is the best in the world; 'tis very rational, and what I have a great value for. But you must not take it ill if I don't use it now.

ELMIRE. [*To* ORGON] Seeing what I see, I don't know what to say; I can but wonder at your blindness. You must be mightily bewitched and prepossessed in his favour, to give us the lie upon the fact of to-day.

ORGON. I am your humble servant, and believe appearances. I

know your complaisance for my rascal of a son, and you were afraid to disavow the trick he would have played the poor man. You were, in a word, too little ruffled to gain credit; you would have appeared to have been moved after a different manner.

ELMIRE.   Is it requisite that our honour should bluster so vehemently at the simple declaration of an amorous transport? Can there be no reply made to what offends us, without fury in our eyes and invectives in our mouth? For my part, I only laugh at such overtures, and the rout made about them by no means pleases me. I love that we should show our discretion with good nature, and cannot like your savage prudes, whose honour is armed with teeth and claws and is for tearing a man's eyes out for a word speaking. Heaven preserve me from such discretion! I would have virtue that is not diabolical, and believe that a denial given with a discreet coldness is no less powerful to give the lover a rebuff.

ORGON.   In short I know the whole affair, and shall not alter my scheme.

ELMIRE.   I admire, still more, at your unaccountable weakness. But what answer could your incredulity make should one let you see that they told you the truth?

ORGON.   See?

ELMIRE.   Ay.

ORGON.   Stuff!

ELMIRE.   But how, if I should contrive a way to let you see it in a very clear light?

ORGON.   A likely story indeed!

ELMIRE.   What a strange man! At least give me an answer. I don't speak of your giving credit to us; but suppose a place could be found where you might see and overhear all, what would you then say of your good man?

ORGON.   In that case, I should say that—I should say nothing, for the thing can't be.

ELMIRE.   You have been too long deluded, and too much have taxed me with imposture. 'Tis necessary that by way of diversion, and without going any farther, I should make you a witness of all they told you.

ORGON.   Do so; I take you at your word. We shall see your address, and how you'll make good your promise.

ELMIRE.   [*To* DORINE] Bid him come to me.

DORINE.   [*To* ELMIRE] He has a crafty soul of his own, and perhaps it would be a difficult matter to surprise him.

ELMIRE.   [*To* DORINE] No, people are easily duped by what they love, and self-love helps 'em to deceive themselves. [*To* CLÉANTE *and* MARIANE] Call him down to me, and do you retire.

Scene IV.

ELMIRE, ORGON.

ELMIRE.   Now do you come and get under this table.
ORGON.   Why so?
ELMIRE.   'Tis a necessary point that you should be well concealed.
ORGON.   But why under this table?
ELMIRE.   Lack-a-day! do as I'd have you, I have my design in my head, and you shall be judge of it. Place yourself there, I tell you, and when you are there, take care that no one either sees or hears you.

ORGON.   I must needs say, I am very complaisant: but I must see you go through your enterprise.

ELMIRE.   You will have nothing, I believe, to reply to me. [*To* ORGON *under the table*] However, as I am going to touch upon a strange affair, don't be shocked by any means. Whatever I may say must be allowed me, as it is to convince you, according to my promise. I am going by coaxing speeches, since I am reduced to it, to make this hypocritical soul drop the mask, to flatter the impudent desires of his love, and give a full scope to his boldness. Since 'tis for your sake alone, and to confound him, that I feign a compliance with his desires, I may give over when you appear, and things need go no farther than you would have them. It lies on you to stop his mad pursuit when you think that matters are carried far enough, to spare your wife, and not to expose me any farther than is necessary to disabuse you. This is your interest, it lies at your discretion, and—He's coming; keep close, and take care not to appear.

Scene V.

TARTUFFE, ELMIRE, ORGON, *still hidden*.

TARTUFFE.   I was told you desired to speak with me here.
ELMIRE.   Yes, I have secrets to discover to you; but pull to that door before I tell 'em you, and look about, for fear of a surprise. [TARTUFFE *goes and shuts the door and returns*] We must not surely make such a business of it as the other was just now. I never was in such a surprise in my whole life: Damis put me into a terrible fright for you, and you saw very well that I did my utmost to baffle his designs and moderate his passion. I was under so much concern, 'tis true, that I had not the thought of contradicting him; but thanks to Heaven, everything was the better for that, and things are put upon a surer footing. The esteem you are in laid that storm, and my husband can have no suspicion of you.

The better to set the rumour of ill tongues at defiance, he desires we should be always together, and from thence it is that without fear of blame I can be locked up with you here alone, and this is what justifies me in laying open to you a heart a little, perhaps, too forward in admitting of your passion.

TARTUFFE. This language, madame, is difficult enough to comprehend, and you talked in another kind of style but just now.

ELMIRE. Alas! if such a refusal disobliges you, how little do you know the heart of a woman! and how little do you know what it means when we make so feeble a defence! Our modesty will always combat, in these moments, those tender sentiments you may inspire us with. Whatever reason we may find for the passion that subdues us, we shall always be a little ashamed to own it. We defend ourselves at first, but by the air with which we go about it, we give you sufficiently to know that our heart surrenders, that our words oppose our wishes for the sake of honour, and that such refusals promise everything. Without doubt this is making a very free confession to you, and having regard little enough to the modesty that belongs to us; but in short, since the word has slipped me, should I have been bent so much upon restraining Damis? Should I, pray, with so much mildness, have hearkened to the offer at large which you made of your heart? Should I have taken the thing as you saw I did, if the offer of your heart had had nothing in it to please me? And when I myself would have forced you to refuse the match which had just been proposed, what is it this instance should have given you to understand but the interest one was inclined to take in you, and the disquiet it would have given me, that the knot resolved on should at least divide a heart which I wanted to have wholly my own?

TARTUFFE. 'Tis no doubt, madame, an extreme pleasure to hear these words from the lips one loves; their honey plentifully diffuses through every sense a sweetness I never before tasted. My supreme study is the happiness of pleasing you, and my heart counts your affection its beatitude; but you must excuse this heart, madame, if it presumes to doubt a little of its felicity. I can fancy these words to be only a sort of artifice to make me break off the match that's upon the conclusion; and if I may with freedom explain myself to you, I shall not rely upon this so tender language till some of the favours which I sigh after, assure me of the sincerity of what may be said, and fix in my mind a firm belief of the transporting goodness you intend me.

ELMIRE. [*Coughing to give her husband notice*] What! proceed so fast? Would you exhaust the tenderness of one's heart at once? One does violence to one's self in making you the most melting declaration; but at the same time this is not enough for you, and one cannot advance so far as to satisfy you unless one pushes the affair to the last favours.

TARTUFFE. The less one deserves a blessing, the less one presumes to hope for it; our love can hardly have a full reliance upon discourses; one easily suspects a condition full fraught with happiness, and one would enjoy it before one believes it. For my particular, who know I so little deserve your favours, I doubt the success of my rashness, and I shall believe nothing, madame, till by realities you have convinced my passion.

ELMIRE. Good lack! how your love plays the very tyrant! What a strange confusion it throws me into! With what a furious sway does it govern the heart! and with what violence it pushes for what it desires! What, is there no getting clear of your pursuit? Do you allow one no time to take breath? Is it decent to persist with so great rigour? To insist upon the things you demand without quarter? To abuse in this manner, by your pressing efforts, the foible you see people have for you?

TARTUFFE. But if you regard my addresses with a favourable eye, why do you refuse me convincing proofs of it?

ELMIRE. But how can one comply with your desires without offending that Heaven which you are always talking of?

TARTUFFE. If nothing but Heaven obstructs my wishes, 'tis a trifle with me to remove such an obstacle, and that need be no restraint upon your love.

ELMIRE. But they so terrify us with the judgments of Heaven!

TARTUFFE. I can dissipate those ridiculous terrors for you, madame; I have the knack of easing scruples. Heaven, 'tis true, forbids certain gratifications. But then there are ways of compounding those matters. It is a science to stretch the strings of conscience according to the different exigences of the case, and to rectify the immorality of the action by the purity of our intention. These are secrets, madame, I can instruct you in; you have nothing to do but passively to be conducted. Satisfy my desire, and fear nothing; I'll answer for you, and will take the sin upon myself. [ELMIRE *coughs loud*] You cough very much, madame.

ELMIRE. Yes, I am on the rack.

TARTUFFE. [*Presenting her with a paper*] Will you please to have a bit of this liquorice?

ELMIRE. 'Tis an obstinate cold, without doubt, and I am satisfied that all the liquorice in the world will do no good in this case.

TARTUFFE. It is, to be sure, very troublesome.

ELMIRE. Ay, more than one can express.

TARTUFFE. In short your scruple, madame, is easily overcome. You are sure of its being an inviolable secret here, and the harm never consists in anything but the noise one makes; the scandal of the world is what makes the offence, and sinning in private is no sinning at all.

ELMIRE. [*After coughing again, and striking upon the table*] In short, I see that I must resolve to yield, that I must consent to grant you everything, and that with less than this I ought not to expect that you should be satisfied or give over. It is indeed very hard to go that length, and I get over it much against my will. But since you are obstinately bent upon reducing me to it, and since you won't believe anything that can be said, but still insist on more convincing testimony, one must e'en resolve upon it and satisfy people. And if this gratification carries any offence in it, so much the worse for him who forces me to this violence; the fault certainly ought not to be laid at my door.

TARTUFFE. Yes, madame, I take it upon myself, and the thing in itself—

ELMIRE. Open the door a little, and pray look if my husband be not in that gallery.

TARTUFFE. What need you take so much care about him? Betwixt us two, he's a man to be led by the nose. He will take a pride in all our conversations, and I have wrought him up to the point of seeing everything without believing anything.

ELMIRE. That signifies nothing; pray go out a little, and look carefully all about.

Scene VI.

ORGON, ELMIRE.

ORGON. [*Coming from under the table*] An abominable fellow, I vow! I can't recover myself; this perfectly stuns me.

ELMIRE. How! do you come out so soon? You make fools of people; get under the table again, stay to the very last, to see things sure, and don't trust to bare conjectures.

ORGON. No, nothing more wicked ever came from Hell.

ELMIRE. Dear heart, you must not believe too lightly; suffer yourself to be fully convinced before you yield, and don't be too hasty for fear of a mistake. [ELMIRE *places* ORGON *behind her*]

Scene VII.

TARTUFFE, ELMIRE, ORGON.

TARTUFFE. [*Not seeing* ORGON] Everything conspires, madame, to my satisfaction. I have surveyed this whole apartment; nobody's there, and my ravished soul— [TARTUFFE *going with open arms to embrace* ELMIRE, *she retires, and* TARTUFFE *sees* ORGON]

ORGON.   [*Stopping* TARTUFFE] Gently, gently; you are too eager in your amours; you should not be so furious. Ah, ha, good man! you intended me a crest, I suppose! Good-lack, how you abandon yourself to temptations! What, you'd marry my daughter, and had a huge stomach to my wife? I was a long while in doubt whether all was in good earnest, and always thought you would change your tone; but this is pushing the proof far enough. I am now satisfied, and want, for my part, no further conviction.

ELMIRE.   [*To* TARTUFFE] The part I have played was contrary to my inclination; but they reduced me to the necessity of treating you in this manner.

TARTUFFE.   [*To* ORGON] What? Do you believe—

ORGON.   Come, pray no noise; turn out, and without ceremony.

TARTUFFE.   My design—

ORGON.   These speeches are no longer in season; you must troop off forthwith.

TARTUFFE.   'Tis you must troop off, you who speaks so magisterially. The house belongs to me; I'll make you know it, and shall plainly show you that you have recourse in vain to these base tricks to pick a quarrel with me; that you don't think where you are when you injure me; that I have wherewithal to confound and punish imposture, to avenge offended Heaven, and make them repent it who talk here of turning me out o' doors.

Scene VIII.

ELMIRE, ORGON.

ELMIRE.   What language is this? And what can it mean?

ORGON.   In truth I'm all confusion, and have no room to laugh.

ELMIRE.   How so?

ORGON.   I see my fault by what he says, and the deed of gift perplexes me.

ELMIRE.   The deed of gift?

ORGON.   Ay, 'tis done; but I have something else that disturbs me too.

ELMIRE.   And what's that?

ORGON.   You shall know the whole; but let's go immediately and see if a certain casket is above stairs.

Act V.

Scene I.

ORGON, CLÉANTE.

CLÉANTE.   Whither would you run?

ORGON.   Alas! how can I tell?

CLÉANTE.   I think we ought, the first thing we do, to consult together what may be done at this juncture.

ORGON.   This casket entirely confounds me. It gives me even more vexation than all the rest.

CLÉANTE.   This casket then is some mystery of importance?

ORGON.   It is a deposit that Argas, my lamented friend, himself committed as a great secret to my keeping. When he fled, he pitched on me for this purpose; and these are the papers, as he told me, whereon his life and fortune depend.

CLÉANTE.   Why then did you trust them in other hands?

ORGON.   Merely out of a scruple of conscience. I went straight to impart the secret to my traitor, and his casuistry over-persuaded me rather to give him the casket to keep; so that to deny it, in case of any inquiry, I might have the relief of a subterfuge ready at hand, whereby my conscience would have been very secure in taking an oath contrary to the truth.

CLÉANTE.   You are in a bad situation, at least, if I may believe appearances; both the deed of gift and the trust reposed are, to speak my sentiments to you, steps which you have taken very inconsiderately. One might carry you great lengths by such pledges; and this fellow having these advantages over you, it is still a great imprudence in you to urge him; and you ought to think of some gentler method.

ORGON.   What! under the fair appearance of such affectionate zeal, to conceal such a double heart, and a soul so wicked? And that I, who took him in poor and indigent—'Tis over, I renounce all pious folks. I

43

shall henceforth have an utter abhorrence of them, and shall become, for their sakes, worse than a devil.

CLÉANTE.   Mighty well; here are some of your extravagances! You never preserve a moderate temper in anything. Right reason and yours are very different, and you are always throwing yourself out of one extreme into another. You see your error and are sensible that you have been imposed on by a hypocritical zeal; but in order to reform, what reason is there that you should be guilty of a worse mistake, and that you should make no difference between the heart of a perfidious worthless wretch and those of all honest people? What! because a rascal has impudently imposed upon you under the pompous show of an austere grimace, will you needs have it that everybody's like him, and that there are no devout people to be found in the world? Leave these foolish consequences to libertines; distinguish between virtue and the appearance of it; never hazard your esteem too suddenly; and, in order to do this, keep the mean you should do. Guard, if possible, against doing honour to imposture; but, at the same time, don't injure true zeal; and if you must fall into one extreme, rather offend again on the other side.

Scene II.

ORGON, CLÉANTE, DAMIS.

DAMIS.   What, sir, is it true that the rascal threatens you? That he has quite forgotten every favour he has received? And that his base abominable pride arms your own goodness against yourself?

ORGON.   Yes, son, and it gives me inconceivable vexation.

DAMIS.   Let me alone, I'll slice both his ears off. There's no dallying with such insolence as his. I'll undertake to rid you of your fears at once; and to put an end to the affair, I must do his business for him.

CLÉANTE.   That's spoken exactly like a young fellow. Pray moderate these violent transports; we live in an age, and under a government, in which violence is but a bad way to promote our affairs.

Scene III.

MME. PERNELLE, ORGON, ELMIRE,
CLÉANTE, MARIANE, DAMIS, DORINE.

MME. PERNELLE.   What's all this? I hear terrible mysteries here.

ORGON.   They are novelties that I am an eye-witness to; you see how finely I am fitted for my care. I kindly pick up a fellow in misery, entertain and treat him like my own brother, heap daily favours on him; I give him my daughter and my whole fortune; when at the same time the perfidious, infamous wretch forms the black design of seducing my wife. And not content with these base attempts, he dares to menace me with my own favours, and would make use of those advantages to my ruin which my too indiscreet good-nature put into his hands, to turn me out of my estate, which I made over to him, and to reduce me to that condition from which I rescued him.

DORINE.   The poor man!

MME. PERNELLE.   I can never believe, son, he could commit so black an action.

ORGON.   How?

MME. PERNELLE.   Good people are always envied.

ORGON.   What would you insinuate, mother, by this discourse?

MME. PERNELLE.   Why, that there are strange doings at your house; and the ill-will they bear him is but too evident.

ORGON.   What has this ill-will to do with what has been told you?

MME. PERNELLE.   I have told you a hundred times when you were a little one,

> That virtue here is persecuted ever;
> That envious men may die, but envy never.

ORGON.   But what is all this to the present purpose?

MME. PERNELLE.   They have trumped up to you a hundred idle stories against him.

ORGON.   I have told you already that I saw it all my own self.

MME. PERNELLE.   The malice of scandal-mongers is very great.

ORGON.   You'll make me swear, mother. I tell you that I saw with my own eyes a crime so audacious—

MME. PERNELLE.   Tongues never want for venom to spit; nothing here below can be proof against them.

ORGON.   This is holding a very senseless argument! I saw it, I say, saw it; with my own eyes I saw it. What you call, saw it. Must I din it a hundred times into your ears, and bawl as loud as four folks?

MME. PERNELLE.   Dear heart! Appearances very often deceive us. You must not always judge by what you see.

ORGON.   I shall run mad.

MME. PERNELLE.   Nature is liable to false suspicions, and good is oftentimes misconstrued evil.

ORGON.   Ought I to construe charitably his desire of kissing my wife?

MME. PERNELLE.   You ought never to accuse anybody but upon

good grounds; and you should have stayed till you had seen the thing certain.

ORGON.   What the devil! How should I be more certain? Then, mother, I should have stayed till he had—You'll make me say some foolish thing or other.

MME. PERNELLE.   In short, his soul burns with too pure a flame, and I can't let it enter my thoughts that he could attempt the things that are laid to his charge.

ORGON.   Go, if you were not my mother I don't know what I might say to you, my passion is so great!

DORINE.   [*To* ORGON] The just return, sir, of things here below. Time was, you would believe nobody, and now you can't be believed yourself.

CLÉANTE.   We are wasting that time in mere trifles which should be spent in taking measures; we shouldn't sleep when a knave threatens.

DAMIS.   What, can his impudence come to this pitch?

ELMIRE.   I can scarce think this instance possible, for my part; his ingratitude would in this be too visible.

CLÉANTE.   [*To* ORGON] Don't you depend upon that. He will be cunning enough to give the colour of reason for what he does against you; and for a less matter than this, the weight of a cabal has involved people in dismal labyrinths. I tell you once again that, armed with what he has, you should never have urged him so far.

ORGON.   That's true; but what could I do in the affair? I was not master of my resentments at the haughtiness of the traitor.

CLÉANTE.   I wish with all my heart that there could be any shadow of a peace patched up between you.

ELMIRE.   Had I but known how well he had been armed, I should never have made such an alarm about the matter, and my—

ORGON.   [*To* DORINE, *seeing* M. LOYAL *coming*] What would that man have? Go quickly and ask. I'm in a fine condition to have people come to see me.

Scene IV.

ORGON, MME. PERNELLE, ELMIRE,
MARIANE, CLÉANTE, DAMIS, DORINE, M. LOYAL.

M. LOYAL.   [*To* DORINE *at the farther part of the stage*] Good-morning, child; pray let me speak to your master.

DORINE.   He's in company, and I doubt he can see nobody now.

M. LOYAL.   Nay, I am not for being troublesome here. I believe my coming will have nothing in it that will displease him; I come upon an affair that he'll be very glad of.

DORINE.   Your name, pray?

M. LOYAL.   Only tell him that I come on the part of Monsieur Tartuffe, for his good.

DORINE.   [To ORGON] 'Tis a man who comes in a civil way upon business from Monsieur Tartuffe, which he says you won't dislike.

CLÉANTE.   [To ORGON] You must see who this man is and what he wants.

ORGON.   [To CLÉANTE] Perhaps he comes to make us friends. How shall I behave myself to him?

CLÉANTE.   Be sure don't be angry, and if he speaks of an agreement you must listen to him.

M. LOYAL.   [To ORGON] Save you, sir! Heaven blast the man who would wrong you, and may it be as favourable to you as I wish.

ORGON.   [Aside to CLÉANTE] This mild beginning favours my conjecture, and already forebodes some accommodation.

M. LOYAL.   I always had a prodigious value for all your family, and was servant to the gentleman your father.

ORGON.   Sir, I am much ashamed, and ask pardon that I don't know you or your name.

M. LOYAL.   My name is Loyal, sir, by birth a Norman, and I am tipstaff to the court in spite of envy. I have had the good fortune for forty years together to fill that office, thanks to Heaven, with great honour. I come, sir, with your leave, to signify to you the execution of a certain decree.

ORGON.   What, are you here—

M. LOYAL.   Sir, without passion, 'tis nothing but a summons, an order to remove hence, you and yours, to take out your goods, and to make way for others, without remission or delay, so that 'tis necessary—

ORGON.   I go from hence?

M. LOYAL.   Yes, sir, if you please. The house at present, as you know but too well, belongs to good Monsieur Tartuffe, without dispute. He is henceforward lord and master of your estate, by virtue of a contract I have in charge. 'Tis in due form, and not to be contested.

DAMIS.   [To M. LOYAL] Most certainly 'tis prodigious impudence, and what I can't but admire!

M. LOYAL.   [To DAMIS] Sir, my business is not with you but [Pointing to ORGON] with this gentleman, who is mild and reasonable, and knows the duty of an honest man too well to oppose authority.

ORGON.   But—

M. LOYAL.   [To ORGON] Yes, sir, I know you would not rebel for a million, and that, like a good honest gentleman, you will suffer me here to execute the orders I have received.

DAMIS. You may chance, Monsieur Tipstaff, to get your black jacket well brushed here.

M. LOYAL. [To ORGON] Either, sir, cause your son to be silent or withdraw. I should be very loath to put pen to paper, and see your names in my information.

DORINE. [Aside] This Monsieur Loyal has a disloyal sort of look with him!

M. LOYAL. I have a great deal of tenderness for all honest people, and should not, sir, have charged myself with these writs but to serve and oblige you and to prevent another's being pitched on, who, not having the love for you which I have, might have proceeded in a less gentle manner.

ORGON. And what can be worse than to order people to go out of their house?

M. LOYAL. Why, you are allowed time. And, till to-morrow, I shall suspend, sir, the execution of the warrant. I shall only come and pass the night here with half a score of my folks, without noise or scandal. For form's sake, if you please, the keys of the door must, before you go to bed, be brought me. I'll take care your rest shan't be disturbed, and suffer nothing that is improper to be done. But to-morrow morning you must be ready to clear the house of even the least utensil. My people shall assist you, and I have picked out a set of lusty fellows that they may do you the more service in your removal. Nobody can use you better, in my opinion; and as I treat you with great indulgence, I conjure you, sir, to make a good use of it and to give me no disturbance in the execution of my office.

ORGON. [Aside] I'd give just now a hundred of the best louis d'ors I have left, for the power and pleasure of laying one sound blow on your ass-ship's muzzle.

CLÉANTE. [Aside to ORGON] Give over; don't let's make things worse.

DAMIS. This impudence is too great; I can hardly refrain; my fingers itch to be at him.

DORINE. Faith, Monsieur Brawny-backed Loyal, some thwacks of a cudgel would by no means sit ill upon you.

M. LOYAL. Those infamous words are punishable, sweetheart; there's law against women too.

CLÉANTE. [To M. LOYAL] Let us come to a conclusion, sir, with this; 'tis enough. Pray give up your paper of indulgence and leave us.

M. LOYAL. Good-bye to ye. Heaven bless you all together!

ORGON. And confound both thee and him that sent thee!

Scene V.

ORGON, MME. PERNELLE, ELMIRE,
CLÉANTE, MARIANE, DAMIS, DORINE.

ORGON.   Well, mother, you see whether I am in the right or no; and you may judge of the rest by the warrant. Do you at length perceive his treacheries?

MME. PERNELLE.   I am stunned, and am tumbling from the clouds.

DORINE.   [To ORGON] You complain without a cause, and blame him wrongfully; this does but confirm his pious intentions. His virtue is made perfect in the love of his neighbour; he knows, very often, that riches spoil the man; and he would only, out of pure charity, take from you everything that may obstruct your salvation.

ORGON.   Hold your tongue. Must I always be repeating that to you?

CLÉANTE.   [To ORGON] Come, let's consult what's proper for you to do.

ELMIRE.   Go and expose the audaciousness of the ungrateful wretch. This proceeding of his invalidates the contract; and his perfidiousness must needs appear too black to let him have the success we are apt to surmise.

Scene VI.

VALÈRE, ORGON, MME. PERNELLE, ELMIRE,
CLÉANTE, MARIANE, DAMIS, DORINE.

VALÈRE.   'Tis with regret, sir, I come to afflict you, but I am constrained to it by the imminence of the danger. A very intimate friend of mine, who knows the interest I ought to take in everything that may concern you, has for my sake violated, by a delicate step, the secrecy due to the affairs of state, and has just sent me advice, the consequence of which reduces you to the expedient of a sudden flight. The rogue who has long imposed on you has thought fit, an hour ago, to accuse you to your prince, and to put into his hands, among other darts he shoots at you, the important casket of a state-criminal, of which, says he, in contempt of the duty of a subject, you have kept the guilty secret. I am not informed of the detail of the crime laid to your charge, but an order is issued out against your person, and to execute it the better, he himself is appointed to accompany the person that is to arrest you.

CLÉANTE.   Now are his pretensions armed, and this is the way that the traitor seeks to make himself master of your estate.

ORGON.   The man, I must own, is a vile animal!

VALÈRE. The least delay may be fatal to you; I have my coach at the door to carry you off, with a thousand louis d'ors that here I bring you. Let's lose no time; the shaft is thrown, and these blows are only parried by flight. I offer myself to conduct you to a place of safety and to accompany you in your escape, even to the last.

ORGON. Alas, what do I not owe to your obliging care! I must take another time to thank you, and I beseech Heaven to be so propitious to me that I may one day acknowledge this generous service. Farewell! Take care, the rest of you—

CLÉANTE. Go quickly; we shall take care, brother, to do what is proper.

Scene VII.

TARTUFFE, POLICE OFFICER, MME. PERNELLE, ORGON, ELMIRE, CLÉANTE, MARIANE, VALÈRE, DAMIS, DORINE.

TARTUFFE. [*Stopping* ORGON] Softly, sir, softly, don't run so fast, you shan't go far to find you a lodging; we take you prisoner in the king's name.

ORGON. Traitor, thou hast reserved this shaft for the last. 'Tis the stroke by which thou art to dispatch me, and this crowns all the rest of thy perfidies.

TARTUFFE. Your abuses have nothing in them that can incense me; I'm instructed to suffer everything for the sake of Heaven.

CLÉANTE. The moderation is great, I must confess.

DAMIS. How impudently the varlet sports with Heaven!

TARTUFFE. All your raving can't move me; I think of nothing but doing my duty.

MARIANE. You have much glory to expect from hence; this employ is a mighty honourable one for you.

TARTUFFE. The employ can't be other than glorious when it proceeds from the power that sent me hither.

ORGON. But do you remember, ungrateful wretch, that my charitable hand raised you from a miserable condition?

TARTUFFE. Yes, I know what succours I might receive from thence, but the interest of my prince is my highest duty. The just obligation whereof stifles in my heart all other acknowledgments; and I could sacrifice to so powerful a tie, friend, wife, kindred, and myself to boot.

ELMIRE. The hypocrite!

DORINE. How artfully he can make a cloak of what is sacred!

CLÉANTE. But if the zeal that puts you on, and with which you trick yourself out, is so perfect as you say it is, how came it not to show itself till he found means of surprising you soliciting his wife? How came you not to think of informing against him till his honour obliged him to drive you out of his house? I don't say that the making over his whole estate to you lately should draw you from your duty; but intending to treat him, as now you do, like a criminal, why did you consent to take anything from him?

TARTUFFE.   [*To the* OFFICER] I beg you, sir, to free me from this clamour, and be pleased to do as you are ordered.

OFFICER.   Yes, 'tis certainly delaying the execution too long. You invite me to fulfil it apropos; and to execute my order, follow me immediately to the prison which we are to allot you for your habitation.

TARTUFFE.   Who? I, sir?

OFFICER.   Yes, you.

TARTUFFE.   Why to prison, pray?

OFFICER.   You are not the person I shall give an account to. [*To* ORGON] Do you, sir, compose yourself after so warm a surprise. We live under a prince who is an enemy to fraud, a prince whose eyes penetrate into the heart, and whom all the art of impostors can't deceive. His great soul is furnished with a fine discernment, and always takes things in a right light; there's nothing gets too much footing by surprise, and his solid reason falls into no excess. He bestows lasting glory of men of worth, but he dispenses his favours without blindness, and his love for the sincere does not foreclose his heart against the horror that's due to those that are otherwise. Even this person was not able to surprise him, and we find he keeps clear of the most subtle snares. He soon pierced through all the baseness contained within his heart. Coming to accuse you, he betrayed himself; and by a just stroke of divine judgment, he discovered himself to be a notorious rogue, of whom His Majesty had received information under another name, the whole detail of whose horrid crimes is long enough to fill volumes of histories. This monarch, in a word, detesting his ingratitude and undutifulness to you, to his other confusions hath added the following, and hath sent me under his direction only to see how far his assurance would carry him and to oblige him to give you full satisfaction. He will moreover that I should strip the traitor of all your papers to which he pretends a right, and give them you. By dint of sovereign power he dissolves the obligation of the contract which gives him your estate, and he pardons moreover this secret offence in which the retreat of your friend involved you; and this recompense he bestows for the zeal he saw you formerly showed in maintaining his rights. To let you see that his heart knows, even when 'tis least expected, how to recompense a good action; that merit with him is never lost, and that he much better remembers good than evil.

DORINE.   May Heaven be praised!

MME. PERNELLE.   Now I begin to revive.

ELMIRE.   Favourable success!

MARIANE.   Who could have foretold this?

ORGON.   [*To* TARTUFFE *as the* OFFICER *leads him off*] Well, traitor, there you are—

Scene VIII.

MME. PERNELLE, ORGON, ELMIRE,
MARIANE, CLÉANTE, VALÈRE, DAMIS, DORINE.

CLÉANTE.   Nay, brother, hold, and don't descend to indignities; leave the wretch to his evil destiny, and don't add to the remorse that oppresses him. Much rather wish that his heart may now happily become a convert to virtue, that he may reform his life through detestation of his crimes, and may soften the justice of a glorious prince; while for his goodness you go and on your knees make the due returns for his lenity to you.

ORGON.   Yes, 'tis well said. Let us, with joy, go throw ourselves at his royal feet, to glory in the goodness which he generously displays to us; then, having acquitted ourselves of this first duty, 'twill be necessary we should apply ourselves, with just care, to another:

> With Hymen's tend'rest joys to crown Valère—
> The generous lover, and the friend sincere.

DOVER · THRIFT · EDITIONS

PLAYS

BOXED SETS